P9-EMG-490

ORLAND PARK PUBLIC LIBRARY
14921 Ravinia Avenue
Orland Park, Illinois 60462
708-428-5100

DISCARD

AUG   2011

Our thanks to the following people
who contributed to the production of
Princess Zelda and the Frog:
Katherine McKeon
Linda Moore
Claude and Tara Gregory
Shelby Boden
Lana Wilkins

A FEIWEL AND FRIENDS BOOK
An Imprint of Macmillan

PRINCESS ZELDA AND THE FROG. Copyright © 2011 by Zelda Wisdom Inc.
All rights reserved. Distributed in Canada by H.B. Fenn and Company Ltd.
Printed in January 2011 in China by South China Printing Co. Ltd., Dongguan
City, Guangdong Province. For information, address Feiwel and Friends,
175 Fifth Avenue, New York, N.Y. 10010.

Library of Congress Cataloging-in-Publication Data Available

ISBN: 978-0-312-60325-0

Feiwel and Friends logo designed by Filomena Tuosto

First Edition: 2011

1 3 5 7 9 10 8 6 4 2

www.feiwelandfriends.com

E
GARDNER,
CAROL

Princess Zelda

and the

Frog

Carol Gardner

Photographs by
Shane Young

Feiwel and Friends
NEW YORK

ORLAND PARK PUBLIC LIBRARY

ONCE UPON A TIME, there lived a princess named Zelda. She was so beautiful, her smile had been known to stop villagers in their tracks.

Princess Zelda lived in a grand castle with her parents, King Sour-Mug and Queen Lucille. They gave her everything a princess could dream of: dazzling jewels, gowns made of the finest silk and satin, scrumptious food, and fantastic toys.

But the one gift they could not give her was . . .

ZZZ

ZZZ

ZZZ

a good night's sleep.

Each night, Princess Zelda would toss and turn, count sheep, and pace the floor. But sleep would not come.

Queen Lucille always said that fresh air might bring rest, so with nothing to lose, Zelda fetched her favorite golden ball and outside she went.

Princess Zelda chased the ball here and there. She kicked the ball far and wide. And then she threw it high into the air. Down, it bounced —**SPLAT!**— right into the middle of a mud puddle.

"**Eww, mud!**" she cried.
"How ever will I get my ball?"
A deep voice answered, "What's
wrong with a little mud, Sparkles?
It's great for unclogging the pores."

Surprised, Princess Zelda looked up.
Sitting on the other side of the
puddle was the ugliest frog she had
ever seen.

"If you must know, this gown is 100% pure silk. That icky mud will ruin it," Princess Zelda explained.

"Maybe I can help, Silky Pants," croaked the frog. "What will you give me if I get your ball?"

"Not a thing!" exclaimed Princess Zelda. "I will get it myself!"

Back to the castle the princess went, and returned wearing a fetching purple bikini.

But when she looked at the mucky puddle, she quickly realized that mud and princesses just don't mix.

Princess Zelda thought for a minute, then said, "If you get my ball, I will give you my crown, my diamond choker, and a gift card for a royal massage."

"No thanks, Sweet Cakes," he said. "However, if you let me eat from your golden bowl, drink from your golden goblet, sleep on your golden bed with my head on your golden pillow, AND promise to be my best friend forever, I will get your ball."

Princess Zelda felt queasy when she heard the frog's request. But she really, really wanted her golden ball back. "I-I-I . . . promise," she stammered.

"Oh, NO!"

"It's a deal, Princess Perfect!" shouted the frog. Then, he jumped—**SPLAT!**—into the mud, picked up the golden ball, and tossed it to the princess.

"**Whoopee!**" cried Princess Zelda. She took the ball and ran all the way back to the castle.

"Wait up, Princess!" the frog called after her. But Princess Zelda was long gone.

560 9 040

That evening as the royal family began dinner, they heard **Flip! Flap! Splosh! Flip! Flap! Splosh!** It sounded like little wet feet climbing up the marble staircase.

Suddenly, there was a knock at the door and a voice cried out,
"Oh, BFF, please let me in! So I might see your lovely grin!"

Princess Zelda ran to the door and opened it. Sure enough, it was the frog from the mud puddle.

"What are you doing here?" she gasped, and slammed the door in the frog's face.

"What is wrong, dear child?" asked Queen Lucille, as the shocked and shaken princess returned to the table. Princess Zelda sadly told her mother the whole story and at that moment . . .

there was another knock.

"Oh, BFF, please let me in!
So I might see your lovely grin!
Remember the promise
  you made to me.
Please let me in—
  we're meant to be!"

"Princess Zelda, you made a
promise. You must let him in,"
said the Queen.

The princess did as she was told. **Flip! Flap! Splosh!**
The frog hopped into the room, over to the table.

"Scooch over so I can eat from your golden bowl," the
frog ordered. Princess Zelda watched in disgust as he ate
and slurped. Snippets of sticky food covered his slimy face.
    "Delicious!" said the frog, letting out a loud burp.
"Can't wait to sack out on your golden bed tonight. See
you later, Sweetums."
    The frog flip-flopped out the door.

After dinner, Princess Zelda burst into her mother's chambers.

"Oh, Mother! How can I share my fine silk bed with such a despicable beast?" she cried.

The Queen grew angry. "A promise is a promise, my dear," she said. "You must keep your word and do as the frog says."

Later that night, as promised,
the frog returned to the castle.

*"Oh, BFF, please let me in!
So I might see your lovely grin!
Remember the promise
you made to me.
Please let me in—we're meant to be!"*

The princess opened the door
and led the frog upstairs to her
royal bedroom.

At first, Princess Zelda tried to offer the frog a plain white pillow made of a perfectly respectable cotton-polyester blend. But the frog kicked up a fuss.

"**Nice try, BFF**. Now let me sleep on your golden bed with your golden pillow, or I'll tell your mother," he warned.

Princess Zelda did as she was asked, and allowed the frog to sleep in her splendid bed.

Instantly, the frog fell asleep and began to snore.

Princess Zelda fumed. "What a vexing noise! I will never get to sleep!" But as she listened to the frog's deep rumbling snore, a feeling of peace washed over her.

And before long, the princess was lulled into a deep sleep herself.

The next morning, Princess Zelda awoke feeling fabulous. Never had she slept so soundly. She turned to thank the frog, but he was gone!

In his place sat a most handsome prince. "Who are you?" she demanded. "And where is the frog?"

"A wicked witch turned me into a frog," the prince explained. "But you kept your promise and were true to your word. You, my BFF, broke the spell!"

Princess Zelda's beautiful smile stretched from ear to ear. She looked at the prince and said,

"Oh, BFF, you were so right.
I used to toss and turn at night.
But with you snoring next to me,
it's plain to see—we're meant to be!"

The End

ORLAND PARK PUBLIC LIBRARY